Peter Porcupine

and the

Peanut Butter Lies

Donna Keith

Illustrated by

Robin Smith

WOODNEATH PRESS

Little Peter Porcupine loves his dad and mother,
But there is something else he loves—creamy peanut butter!

Most days he's quick to listen and chooses to obey,
Yet, there are days he struggles; this was one of those days.

A happy Peter Porcupine woke from dreamy slumber
With thoughts of peanut butter to fill his growing hunger.

Peter's mother, however, had scrambled eggs instead.
"No eggs, please," he said, "just peanut butter on bread!"

"Son," said his mother, "these eggs are good for you,
And you need to eat fruits and vegetables, too.

This bark is quite tasty;
these berries are sweet.
Your breakfast is ready.
Please sit in your seat."

Peter climbed in his chair and tearfully said grace,
Then a taste of the eggs put a smile on his face.

"Though they're good," Peter thought,
"I don't want eggs today."
When he started to speak, he soon got carried away....

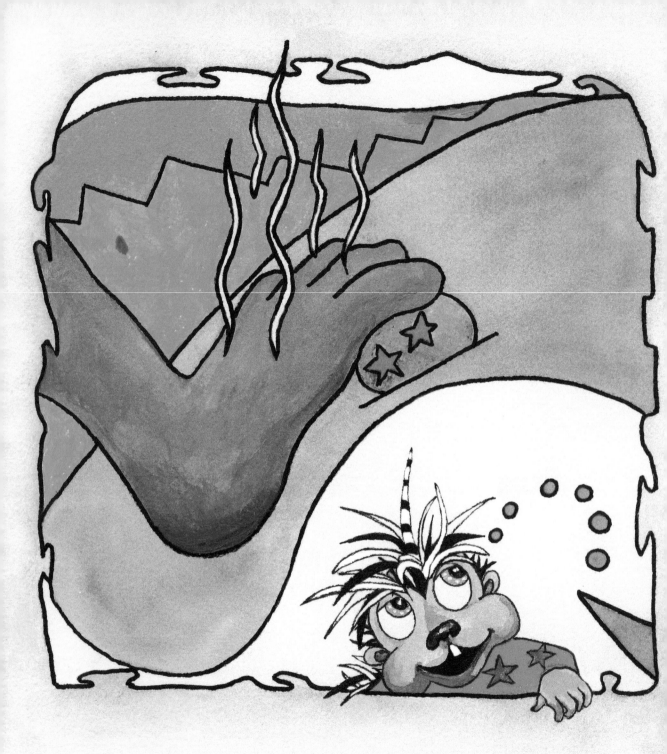

"Mother," he said, "these eggs are not good to eat
Because they could make me have real smelly feet;

And berries might make me run into the road
Or hop and croak like a fat, warty toad."

Mother looked at her son with shock in her eyes.
She was not used to Peter telling her lies.

Still, she pulled up a chair, sat down by her son
To listen once more to the tales being spun.

"If I eat this bark and vegetables now,
It's possible I will moo like a cow!"

lake
fish
bird

"Or," Peter said, "I might chirp like the birds
And forget how to spell my school spelling words!"

The last fib that Peter decided to utter
He hoped would reward him with fresh peanut butter.

"Mother, I don't think that I should eat leaves.
They might cause my arms to shrink into my sleeves."

Now Mother was not fooled
by Peter's tall tales
And decided his plan
would no longer prevail.

"Peter," she sighed, "though you weep and you wail,
This fibbing to get peanut butter will fail."

"I love you, dear Peter, and so does your dad.
These fibs you've been telling have made my heart sad.

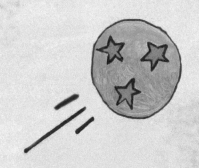

I think time alone in your room may help you
Figure out the right things to say and to do."

Peter fled to his room
and sprawled on the floor,
Then thought of those lies
he had conjured once more.

Soon the ache in his heart
made him kneel down to pray.
When his mother peeked in,
she heard Peter say,

"Dear Jesus, I'm sorry
for lying just then.
I've learned in the Bible
that lying's a sin.

But sometimes I do things
to get my own way
When I should just listen
and choose to obey."

Peter thought of the eggs and the other good food
And decided he'd been a rather rude dude.

"Those eggs Mother fixed will help me grow strong.
I guess I need to admit I was wrong."

Then Peter looked up. "I'm sorry," he said.
"You're forgiven," said Mother as she kissed his head.

"And though you can't live on peanut butter alone,
For lunch you may have some on a crunchy pine cone."

So Peter did.

Scriptures:

Matthew 4:4 "Jesus answered, 'It is written: "Man does not live on bread alone, but on every word that comes from the mouth of God."'"

The Holy Bible: New International Version. Grand Rapids, MI: Zondervan, 2005.

Colossians 3:9a "Dot not lie to each other." (NIV)

The Holy Bible: New International Version. Grand Rapids, MI: Zondervan, 2005.

Dedications

To Isaiah, my peanut butter loving grandson.
Love,
Mammy

To Harrison, my first grandson,

may you always let your imagination run free.

Love,

Nana

The author would like to thank the Kansas City Zoo for providing the following information about their two porcupines--
South American and African Crested porcupine.

The South American prehensile-tailed porcupine is the smaller of the two, averaging about 10 lbs. It lives alone in trees and has a prehensile tail it uses to grab and hang from tree limbs. This porcupine has a spongy pink nose and more personality than the African Crested porcupine. It will come to the ground once a day to urinate. In the wild, it eats leaves, flowers, chutes, roots, bark and the underlayer of trees. At the zoo, it is fed grains, fruits, and vegetables. Jaguars are the main predator of the South American porcupine.

The African Crested porcupine weighs up to 13 lbs, has bigger quills, and lives in family groups of one to four porcupines. It lives mostly on the ground and, in the wild, will forage for up to nine miles at night in search of food, feeding mostly on tubers, bulbs of plants, and fallen fruit. It is a more aggressive porcupine and will back into you if it feels threatened.

CPSIA information can be obtained
at www.ICGtesting.com
Printed in the USA
LVHW07n0123150318
569931LV00004B/11/P